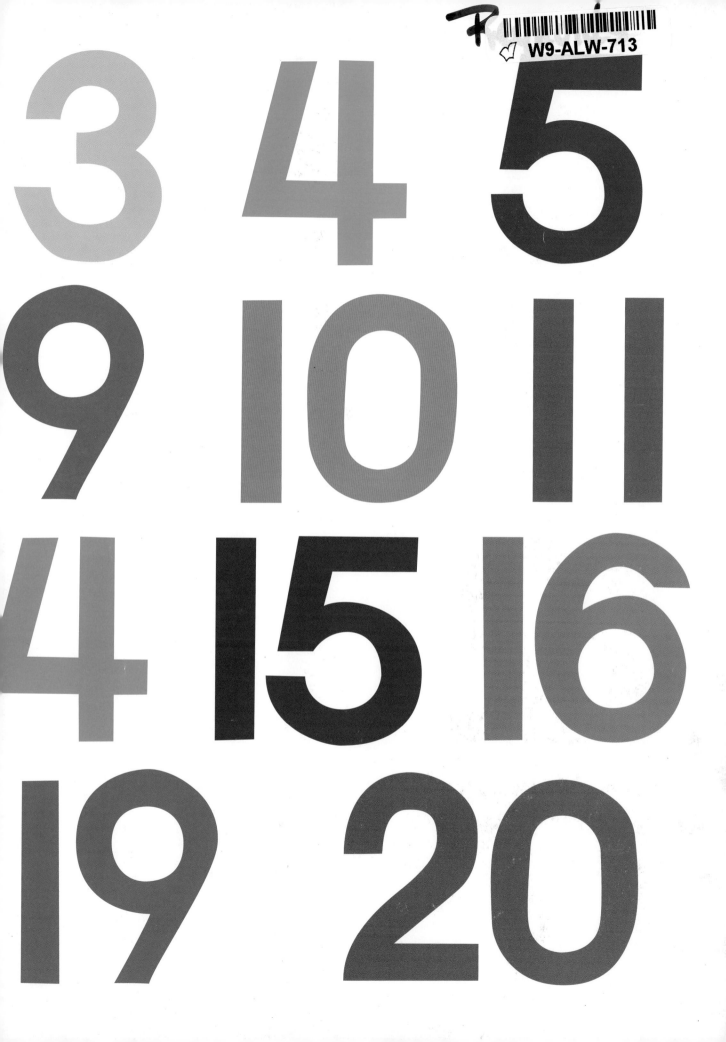

Chicka
Chicka

For Rick Selvaggi—B. M.
For Leslie Pinkham—M. S.
For Libby and Liza, Helen
and Morris—L. E.

Thanks to Lisa van Drasek.

SIMON & SCHUSTER BOOKS FOR YOUNG READERS
An imprint of Simon & Schuster Children's Publishing Division
1230 Avenue of the Americas, New York, New York 10020
Text copyright © 2004 by Bill Martin Jr and
Michael Sampson
Illustrations copyright © 2004
by Lois Ehlert
This work is based on *Chicka Chicka Boom Boom,*
written by Bill Martin Jr and John Archambault
and illustrated by Lois Ehlert.
SIMON & SCHUSTER BOOKS
FOR YOUNG READERS
is a trademark
of Simon & Schuster, Inc.
The text for this book
is set in Bembo.
The illustrations for this
book are rendered
in cut Pantone-
coated papers.
Manufactured in
China

1·2·3

Bill Martin Jr
Michael Sampson
Lois Ehlert

Simon & Schuster Books for Young Readers
New York   London   Toronto   Sydney

Library of Congress Cataloging-in-Publication Data
Martin, Bill, 1916–
Chicka chicka 1, 2, 3 / Bill Martin Jr &
Michael Sampson;
illustrated by Lois Ehlert.—
1st ed.   p. cm.
Summary: Numbers from one
to one hundred climb to the
top of an apple tree in this
rhyming chant.
ISBN-13: 978-1-4169-7501-4
ISBN-10: 1-4169-7501-2
[1. Counting. 2. Stories in
rhyme.] I. Title:
Chicka chicka
one, two, three.
II. Sampson, Michael R.
III. Ehlert, Lois, ill.
IV. Title.
PZ8.3.M3988
Ch 2004
[E]—dc22
2003019106

1 told **2**
and **2** told **3,**
"I'll race you to the top
of the apple tree."

"Climb," said **4**
to **5** and **6,**
bright little numbers
that join the mix.

"Hurry!" yelled **7**
to number **8,**
slow-poke fellow
who's always late.

"Chicka Chicka
1, 2, 3 . . .
Will there be a
place for me?"

Here comes **9**
to the apple tree.
Next comes **10**
and then **11**.
"Wow, these apples
taste like heaven!"

"Chicka Chicka
1, 2, 3 . . .
Will there be a
place for me?"

Hot pink **12,**
lucky **13,**
picking apples
red and green.

14, 15 . . .
Can't you see?
They all want to climb
the apple tree.

"Chicka Chicka
1, 2, 3 . . .
Will there be a
place for me?"

16's next
to make the scene,
climbing branches
with **17**.

18, 19,
one more's **20**.
Numbers, numbers,
there are plenty.

"Chicka Chicka
1, 2, 3 . . .
Will there be a
place for me?"

20.0

Curvy **30,**
flat–foot **40**
climbing up
to join the party!

50's fine
and **60**'s dandy.
70's hair
is long and sandy.

30

"Chicka Chicka
1, 2, 3 . . .
Will there be a
place for me?"

"Let's climb more,"
says treetop **80,**
higher and higher,
up to **90,**

until at last there's **99,**
and all the numbers
are feeling fine,

except for **0,**
who begins to cry.

"Chicka Chicka
1, 2, 3 . . .
Will there be a
place for me?"

Oh, no!

Buzzing close!
Bumblebees!

0 hides
behind the tree.

"GET OUT OF OUR TREE!"
the bumblebees shout,
and all the numbers
tumble out.

90, 80,
70 fall,
hit the ground
in a free-for-all.

60, 50,
40 run.
No more climbing,
no more fun!

30 next,
then sweet little **20**.
Numbers, numbers,
no longer plenty!

19 and **18,**
my, oh my!
Frightened numbers
jump and fly!

17, 16,
15 more.
Now **14** has hit the
floor.

And **13,** too—
unlucky guy!
12 had almost
touched the sky!

Bent-up **11**.
(Wait! Where's **10**?)
9, 8, 7
follow then.

Twisted **6**
and top-hat **5**,
4, 3, 2, 1
take a dive!

"Chicka Chicka
1, 2, 3 . . .
Now I know
the place for me!"

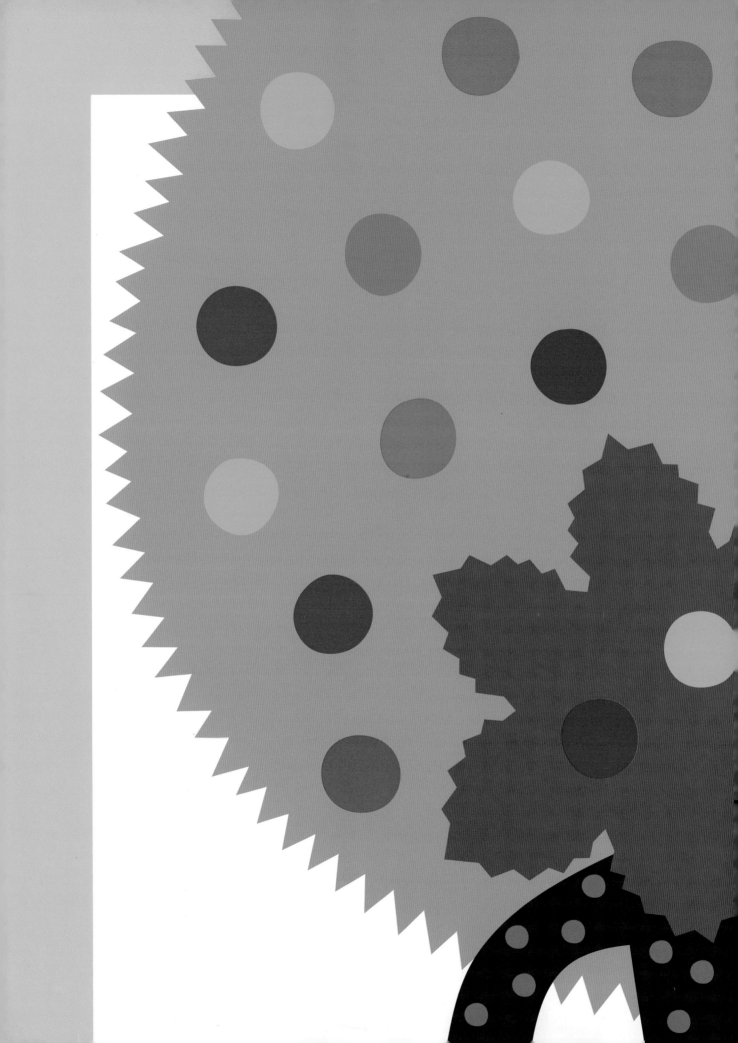

0 leaps into the sky.
Brave little number,
he's not shy.

0 lands on top
of the tree,
joins with **10**.
Now **100** you see!

10

"Chicka Chicka
1, 2, 3 . . .
Here's the place
that's just for me!"

All the numbers
come back out,
higher and higher,
as they shout . . .

"Chicka, Chicka
1, 2, 3!
0's hero of the
number tree!"

0 1 2 3 4 5 6 7 8 9

17 18 19 20 21 22 23

30 31 32 33 34 35

42 43 44 45 46 47

54 55 56 57 58 59

66 67 68 69 70 7

78 79 80 81 82 83

90 91 92 93 94 95